Sincerity

THE BOY WHO CRIED WOLF

Adapted by Janet Quinlan

Illustrated by Jon Goodell

Copyright © 2005 Publications International, Ltd.
All rights reserved.

This publication may not be reproduced in whole or in part by any means whatsoever without written permission from

Louis Weber, C.E.O., Publications International, Ltd., 7373 North Cicero Avenue, Lincolnwood, Illinois 60712

Ground Floor, 59 Gloucester Place, London W1U 8JJ

www.pilbooks.com

Permission is never granted for commercial purposes.

8 7 6 5 4 3 2 1

ISBN 1-4127-3760-5

Once upon a time there was a boy who lived in a village. Although he wasn't very old, he had an important job. He was a shepherd, and it was his responsibility to guard the village sheep from danger, especially from wolves.

The shepherd boy also made sure the sheep got plenty of food and exercise. Each day he took them to a nearby valley. Once they had walked there, the sheep would graze on the tasty green grass that grew in the valley.

The villagers counted on the shepherd boy to take good care of the sheep. They never checked on him because they trusted him to do his job well.

Sometimes it was lonely for the boy to be out all day with only the sheep for company. But he knew he wasn't really alone. The village people worked nearby. If a wolf ever did attack, the people could run to the rescue.

Every day, the shepherd faithfully watched the sheep. From his lookout post, he could see other people hard at work. Some days they worked at their jobs in the village. Sometimes they did other chores. The shepherd boy would sigh. For him every day was the same.

Sometimes the boy wished that something exciting would happen. In his whole life, he had never seen a wolf come near the sheep. In fact, he had never seen a wolf at all!

One day the wind ruffled the leaves on some low trees near his post. "I wonder," he said, thoughtfully, "what is on the other side of those trees?"

The boy smiled to himself. Would it be so bad to pretend there was a wolf? He thought it would be a good joke.

As the sheep ate the grass, he cupped his hand near his mouth and shouted, "Wolf! Wolf! A wolf is stealing the sheep! Come help me!"

All the village people stopped what they were doing and ran to scare away the wolf. When they arrived, they were very confused.

The villagers did not find a wolf. And where was the shepherd? They were worried about him. What if the wolf had stolen the boy? They began to search high and low for him.

A villager pointed to a tree and said, "There he is, over there." They saw he was not hurt. In fact, he was laughing!

"You looked very funny running up here. This was a great joke," laughed the boy.

The villagers did not laugh. They had been very frightened about the boy and the sheep. They shook their heads and said, "We have to go back to work. We don't have time for pranks."

The shepherd boy hardly heard a word they said. He was laughing too hard.

At breakfast the next day, the boy's mother and father were stern. They reminded him how much trouble his lie had caused the villagers. He nodded his head and left to tend the sheep. He meant to be good, but soon he was bored again.

"Wolf! Wolf!" he shouted, louder than the day before. "A wolf is stealing the sheep! Come help me!"

Again the villagers came running. Again there was no wolf in sight. This time the villagers were very upset. They told the boy, "If you don't tell people the truth, they will never know when to believe you."

The boy was still laughing at his joke. After the villagers went back to their jobs, however, he thought about what the people had said. "Maybe," he thought, "it isn't so funny to play tricks on others." The shepherd boy began walking back to his lookout post. Little did he know that soon he was going to have all the excitement he could handle.

On the other side of the trees lurked a hungry wolf. When the shepherd reached his post, the wolf sprang from his hiding place and ran toward the sheep. The shepherd couldn't believe his eyes. It was a real wolf! He cried out, "Wolf! Wolf! A wolf is stealing the sheep! Come help me!"

He waited for the villagers to come running, but no one came. They weren't going to fall for that trick again. But this time, it wasn't a trick.

The poor sheep bleated and rolled their eyes. They ran in confused circles as the wolf herded them through the trees and into the forest.

The boy tried yelling for help again, but still no one came. He could see the wolf rounding up the last of the sheep. Where were the villagers? He needed their help!

The shepherd boy felt like crying. What should he do? He could never catch the wolf by himself. He had to find the villagers.

The shepherd ran into the village. "Wolf! Wolf!" he cried, breathlessly. "He's stealing our sheep! " The boy kept running and calling for help, but no one believed he was telling the truth. He called out again, "Wolf! Wolf! Please help me!"

"Yeah, right!" said one villager. "I can't believe that boy is trying to make fools out of us again."

"Well, he's not going to make a fool out of me," said another villager. "I don't believe him."

Finally, the shepherd boy stopped running. "I'm telling the truth this time!" he shouted. "There really is a wolf in the valley, and he's stealing the sheep. You've got to believe me."

The villagers frowned at the boy. They shook their fingers at him. "We're smarter than you think," the people said. "This time we're going to ignore you and your wolf! You fooled us before, but you're not going to fool us again. Harrumph!"

The shepherd boy was crushed. He knew that there was no way to make the villagers believe that he was telling the truth. And how could he blame them? He had lost their trust by playing tricks on them.

He walked slowly back to his lookout and gazed down at the spot where he had always taken his sheep to graze. Now there were no sheep left; the wolf had stolen them all. The boy sat down on the grass. Tears of frustration and sadness ran down his cheeks.

The young shepherd remembered what his parents and the villagers had told him. How he wished he had listened to what they said! Telling the truth would have saved him and the rest of the villagers so much grief.

Although he could not help the sheep, the boy learned an important lesson that day. He vowed always to tell the truth. Over time, he was even able to regain the trust of the villagers, and his sincerity was never doubted again.

Sincerity

Being sincere means acting honestly. In this story, when the shepherd boy pretends there is a wolf near his sheep, he thinks it is a funny joke. The villagers, on the other hand, are angry that he has lied to them.

Later, when a wolf does attack the sheep, the villagers do not believe the shepherd is being sincere when he calls for help. They no longer trust him. The shepherd is sad to lose the sheep. He realizes that if he had always been honest, the villagers would never have had reason to doubt him.